DRAGONBLOOD

THE GIRL WHO BREATHED FIRE

BY MICHAEL DAHL

ILLUSTRATED BY

a capstone imprint

Zone Books are published by
Stone Arch Books
A Capstone Imprint
151 Good Counsel Drive, P.O. Box 669
Mankato, Minnesota 56002
www.capstonepub.com

Library of Congress Cataloging-in-Publication Data is
available on the Library of Congress website.

Library binding: 978-1-4342-1925-1

Art Director: Kay Fraser
Graphic Designer: Hilary Wacholz
Production Specialist: Michelle Biedscheid

TABLE OF CONTENTS

Introduction

A new Age of Dragons is about to begin. The **powerful** creatures will return to rule the **world** once more, but this time will be different. This time, they will have allies. Who will help them? Around the world, some young humans are making a strange discovery. They are learning that they were born with dragon blood – blood that gives them **amazing powers**.

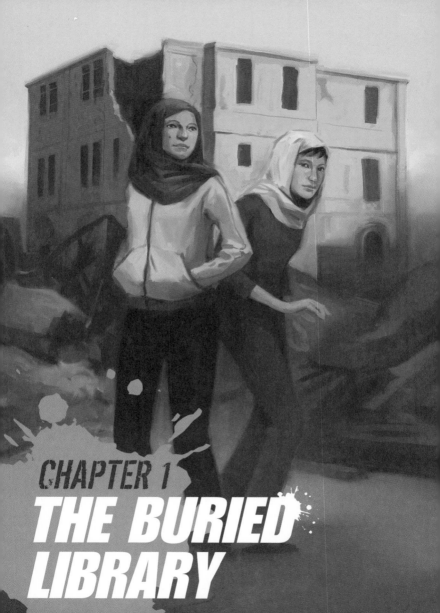

CHAPTER 1
THE BURIED LIBRARY

In the Middle East, two girls wandered through a **crumbling** building.

Farah and Noor helped each other **climb** over fallen stones.

A tunnel led them **DEEPER** into the building.

"Are you sure there is something to eat in here?" asked Noor.

The girls *walked* down several dark hallways.

They turned a corner and Farah **clapped** her hands together. "I knew it was here," she said happily.

Noor looked ⬆ **UP**.

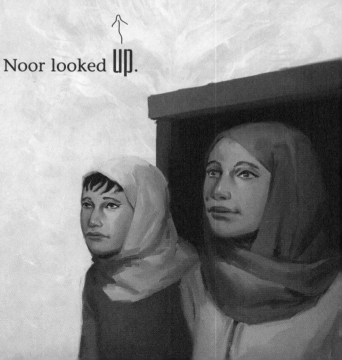

The room was  of books.

"It's a library!" said Noor.
"Our families need food, Farah."

"This is **better** than food,"
said Farah.

"This is the library my mother
and I used to visit," she said.
"Before the **WAR**."

Farah began searching through the shelves. She climbed over rubble and **broken** furniture.

A ray of sunlight fell through a hole high above them.

Noor stood in the light and rubbed her arms. She was cold.

"Look!" cried Farah. "It is still here."

She held a **HUGE** book with covers that looked like stone.

Then Farah looked at her friend.

"You are in this book," Farah said.

CHAPTER 2
A PAINTED DRAGON

Noor climbed up beside her friend and looked at the **book**.

"Look at this," said Farah.

She pointed to a painting on a yellowed page.

It was a dragon with a **curling** tail. Fire blasted from the dragon's jaws.

Noor **stared** hard at the painting. She began to **tremble.**

"It looks like your **BIRTHMARK**," said Farah.

Years ago, when they were both little, Noor had shown Farah her **strange** birthmark. It covered her right arm.

The birthmark was **HARD** for Noor to look at.

Farah had always called it "Noor's **DRAGON**."

Now, Noor was **frightened**.

She stood up. "No, that's not it!"
she yelled. "You are wrong!"

Thud! Thud! Thud!

The girls heard footsteps echo down the **dark** hall.

CHAPTER 3
SOLDIERS

A strange man's voice rang through the library.

"Someone else is in here!" he called.

Noor and Farah ducked BEHIND a bookshelf.

Just then, three **soldiers** stepped out of the shadows.

One of the soldiers *quickly* spotted the girls.

"What are you doing in here?" he shouted.

"I'm sorry," said Farah. "We were only looking for food. Our families are hungry."

"We did not mean to trespass," she added. "We will leave right now."

"Stay right where you are!" shouted the first soldier again.

He gripped his WEAPON.

Noor's mouth felt DRY.

She could NOT speak.

Farah **dropped** the book she
was holding.

She pointed at Noor and gasped.
"Your breath!" she said.

Pale flames were **spurting**
from Noor's mouth.

CHAPTER 4
THE PROTECTOR

The soldiers stepped back in fear. They **raised** their weapons.

A roar **shattered** the air.

Noor was gone. In her place stood a **DRAGON** with a curling tail.

Flames shot from its open jaws.

One of the men **aimed** his weapon at the creature's heart.

Farah SCREAMED.

Suddenly, a great **stream** of fire shot from the dragon's mouth.

The **DARK** chamber blazed with light.

The blaze quickly vanished.
SMOKE hung in the silent air.

Farah looked for the soldiers, but
they were gone. All she saw were
puddles of **melted metal**.

Farah heard a soft Sound in the shadows.

Noor was **sobbing** into her hands.

"You saved us, Noor!" Farah said.

"You saved us!"

Noor looked **up**.

"Let's go home," she said.

Farah **nodded** and helped her
friend to her feet.

Quickly, without looking back,
the two girls headed out into the
long, dark **HALLWAY**.

Dragons in Popular Culture

In 1959, Walt Disney released the movie *Sleeping Beauty*. In the movie, the **EVIL** fairy turns herself into a dragon. The dragon scenes were very costly to make. The film almost made the Disney studio go bankrupt. However, the film is now considered one of the **best** animated movies ever made. It was re-released in 2008.

Since the first **animated** dragon in *Sleeping Beauty*, many children's movies feature dragons. Many of them are nice dragons. Both *Mulan* and *Shrek* have friendly dragons.

In the 1960s, the popular folk group Peter, Paul, and Mary recorded a **song** called "Puff the Magic Dragon." In 2007, the song was made into a children's book and became a bestseller.

A game called Dungeons and Dragons was released in 1973. It became a huge success. Books and movies were created based on the game.

In 1999, a children's show called "Dragon Tales" became popular. It was about siblings who went to Dragon Land and had lots of fun adventures.

One of the first movies to create a "LIVE" dragon was *Dragonslayer* in 1981. Since then, movie dragons have become more real looking.

ABOUT THE AUTHOR

Michael Dahl is the author of more than 200 books for children and young adults. He has won the AEP Distinguished Achievement Award three times for his nonfiction. His Finnegan Zwake mystery series was shortlisted twice by the Anthony and Agatha awards. He has also written the Library of Doom series. He is a featured speaker at conferences around the country on graphic novels and high-interest books for boys.

ABOUT THE ILLUSTRATOR

After getting a graphic design degree and working as a designer for a couple of years, Federico Piatti realized he was spending way too much time drawing and painting, and too much money on art books and comics, so his path took a turn toward illustration. He currently works creating imagery for books and games, mostly in the fantasy and horror genres. Argentinian by birth, he now lives in Madrid, Spain, with his wife, who is also an illustrator.

GLOSSARY

birthmark (BURTH-mark)—a mark on the skin that has been present since birth

blaze (BLAYZ)—a fierce fire

blazing (BLAYZ-ing)—burning fiercely

chamber (CHAYM-bur)—a room

creature (KREE-chur)—a living being

crumbling (KRUM-buhl-ing)—breaking into small pieces

rubble (RUHB-uhl)—broken bricks and stones

soldiers (SOLE-jurz)—people in an army

tremble (TREM-buhl)—to shake

trespass (TRESS-pass)—enter without permission

weapon (WEP-uhn)—something that can be used in a fight

yellowed (YEL-ohd)—made yellow with age

DISCUSSION QUESTIONS

1. Farah had hints of Noor's **powers**, but Noor didn't want to think about it. Why was she <u>scared</u> of her own power?

2. If Noor and Farah were looking for food, why was Farah so excited to find the **library?**

3. Did Noor do the right thing when she turned into a **DRAGON?** Explain your answer.

WRITING PROMPTS

1. Noor and Farah are **best** friends. Write about your closest friend. What do you like about that person? Why are you so close? **? ? ?**

2. Were you **surprised** by the ending? Write a paragraph describing what you thought would happen at the end.

3. What would you do if you **discovered** that one of your friends was secretly a dragon? How would you react? Write about it.